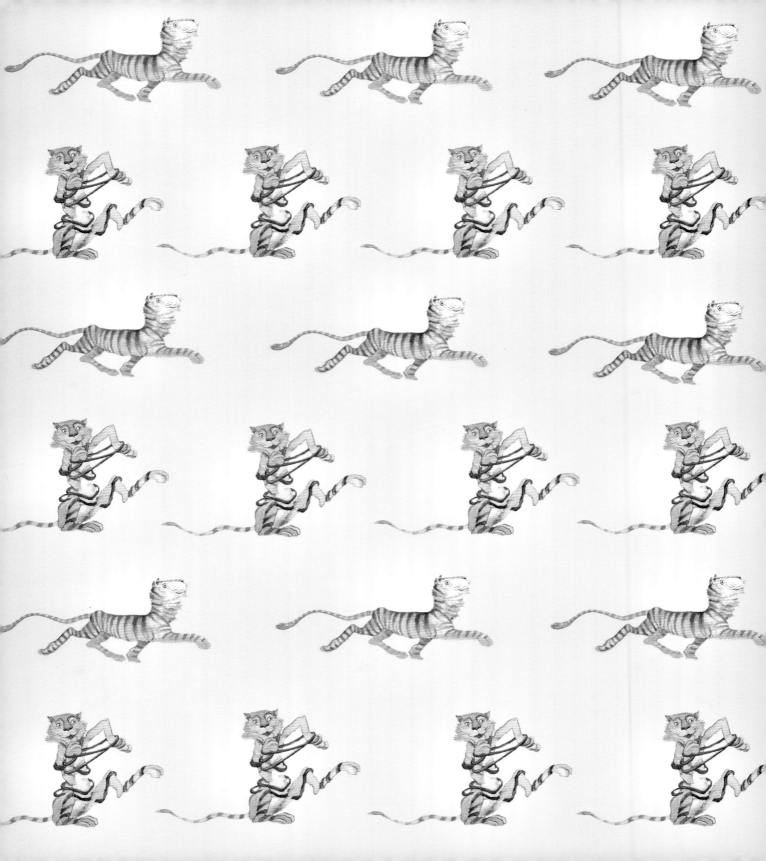

The Tiger Who Lost His Stripes

ISBN 0 86264 597 2

This edition published in Great England in 1995 by Andersen Press Ltd.

Text © 1995 by Anthony Paul.

Illustrations © 1995 by Michael Foreman.

First published in 1980.

失去斑紋的老虎

Anthony Paul 著

Michael Foreman 繪

柯美玲 譯

三民書局

General MacTiger was the most **magnificent** animal in the forest. He had **splendid** whiskers, flashing eyes and a **stately** walk. Most specially he had a thick silky coat with **dazzling** black **stripes**.

general [`dʒɛnərəl] 名 將軍
magnificent [mæg`nıfəsṇt] 形 高雅的
splendid [`splɛndəd] 形 閃亮眩目的
stately [`stetlı] 形 有威嚴的
dazzling [`dæzlıŋ] 形 耀眼的
stripe [straıp] 名 條紋

　　麥大虎將軍是森林裡最高貴、最美麗的動物。亮晶晶的鬍鬚、會發光的眼睛，走起路來好神氣。最特別的是，他身上穿著一件光滑柔軟的厚外套，上面還有一條一條閃閃發亮的黑色斑紋，漂亮極了。

But one morning when the General took a look at himself in the river he had a **horrible shock**. He was all yellow! His stripes had gone!

This was a serious business. How could he be a tiger without any stripes? A tiger's whole tigerishness is in his stripes.

So what did he do? Did he sit down and cry? Certainly not! A tiger never cries. Did he get himself into a **terrific thundering rage**? Well, he almost did, but he stopped himself, remembering that he was General MacTiger, who was always **dignified** and stately.

horrible [`hɔrəbḷ] 形 可怕的
shock [ʃɑk] 名 衝擊
terrific [tə`rɪfɪk] 形 激烈的
thundering [`θʌndərɪŋ] 形 雷鳴似的
rage [redʒ] 名 憤怒
dignified [`dɪgnə,faɪd] 形 高貴的

　　有一天早上，麥將軍跑到河邊照鏡子。他往河面一看。天啊！他竟然變成一隻純黃色的老虎，身上的斑紋全不見了！

　　這是一個嚴重的問題。身為老虎，怎麼可以沒有斑紋呢？老虎就是因為身上的斑紋才叫老虎啊！

　　你猜他怎麼樣？有沒有坐在地上嚎啕大哭？當然沒有！老虎怎麼能掉眼淚呢！那麼他有沒有大發雷霆呢？嗯，差一點點，不過他還是忍了下來。他告訴自己：「我是麥大虎將軍，高貴、穩重的麥大虎將軍。」

So he kept calm, and said to himself, "**By George**, what a **remarkable** case of stripelessness! I must **get to the bottom of** it." And off he went to look for his stripes.

He looked in the long grass, in the reeds, in the bamboo groves. But not a **sniff** of those stripes could he find.

After hours of searching General MacTiger **plodded** home. By now he didn't feel at all like himself. He wondered if he had somehow been changed into a different animal altogether, some yellow stranger. He didn't like this idea at all.

by George　的確
remarkable [rɪˋmɑrkəb!] 形 值得注意的
get to the bottom of... 查明…的真相
sniff [snɪf] 名 氣味
plod [plɑd] 動 步伐沈重地行走

　　他冷靜下來對自己說：「說實在的，丟掉斑紋可不是件小事。我得查出真相。」於是他便出發去尋找他的斑紋。

　　他找遍了牧草區、蘆葦田、竹子林，可是怎麼聞，就是沒有斑紋的味道。

　　找了一個小時又一個小時，最後麥大虎垂頭喪氣地走回家。他一點也不喜歡自己現在的樣子。他心想：「我會不會變成另外一種動物了？一種我從沒見過的黃色動物。」一想到這裡，他就覺得好難過。

Trudging sadly along, he saw something **odd** hanging from a branch, a sort of bag or basket made of stripes of dark stuff. Was it a wasps' nest? Was it a sock? General MacTiger looked, and he looked, and,

"MY STRIPES!!" **roared** General MacTiger.

From the basket-thing **slid** a flat head at the end of a long neck that wasn't exactly a neck. It was the **python**. In a dry **whispery** voice the python said, "Can't you make less noise?"

"Fury! Roar! Robber!" thundered the General.

"It's no good roaring," said the python. "Once I get my hands on something I hang on to it."

"But you haven't got any hands," said General MacTiger.

"So what," whispered the python, and slid back inside the basket-thing.

trudge [trʌdʒ] 動 有氣無力地走
odd [ɑd] 形 奇怪的
roar [rɔr] 動 吼叫
slide [slaɪd] 動 滑
python [ˋpaɪθɑn] 名 蟒蛇
whispery [ˋhwɪspərɪ] 形 沙沙作響的

　　麥大虎有氣無力地走在路上，心裡難過極了。突然，他看見一棵樹上掛著一個好奇怪的東西，好像袋子又好像籃子，外面還包著一條條黑色的東西。那是黃蜂的巢嗎？還是一隻短襪？麥大虎將軍左看右看…

　　「我的斑紋！」他突然大吼一聲。

　　這時從那個籃子般的東西溜出一顆扁扁的頭，後面還接著長長的，好像脖子又不太像脖子的東西。原來是條大蟒蛇。大蟒蛇用沙啞的聲音對他說：「你能不能安靜一點？」

　　「潑婦！兇婆娘！強盜！」麥大虎罵得好大聲。

　　「你大吼大叫做什麼，」大蟒蛇說。「只要是我拿到的東西，我絕不放手。」

　　「可是你又沒有手！」麥大虎說。

　　「要你管，」大蟒蛇頂回去，說完便溜回那個籃子般的東西。

After a minute or so the General said, "Look here, python, what are you doing with my stripes? You must give them back to me."

"**What if** I don't?" said the python.

"If you don't? — If you don't — I'll be very angry indeed!"

"How terrible," said the python. "I'll have to put my earplugs in. I hate loud noises."

General MacTiger made a sound like a bath emptying. Then he said, "Earplugs? But you haven't got any ears!"

"And you haven't got any stripes," said the python, and slid back inside the basket-thing. General MacTiger stood there with his mouth hanging open.

What if...? 　如果…將會怎麼樣？

10
11

大約過了一分鐘，麥大虎將軍又說話了：「大蟒蛇，你給我聽著。你拿我的斑紋做什麼？趕快還給我！」

「如果我不還呢？」大蟒蛇說。

「如果你不還——如果你不還——我就會非常非常生氣！」

「好可怕唷！」大蟒蛇說，「看來我得趕快用耳塞把耳朵塞住。我最怕吵了。」

麥大虎將軍大吼一聲，那聲音好像浴缸裡的水快要排光，有點空洞。他說：「耳塞？可是你沒有耳朵啊！」

「那你也沒有斑紋啊！」大蟒蛇說完，又溜回那個籃子般的東西。麥大虎將軍愣在那兒，嘴巴張得好大。

General MacTiger had a good think, then he called out, "Hey, python! What can I **swap** you **for** those stripes?"

"Swap?" said the python. "Well I like this house, but I **suppose** I might swap it for an even better one."

"What sort of better one?" said the General.

"Oh, a good strong one of elephant grass would do."

"Elephant grass?" said General MacTiger. "How can I build a house of elephant grass?"

"I don't know. Ask the elephants," said the python.

swap [swap] 動 交換
swap (sb.) for (sth.) 與（人）交換（物）
suppose [səˋpoz] 動 認為

麥大虎想了好一會兒，然後又開口了：「嗨，大蟒蛇，我要拿什麼來，才能跟你交換那些斑紋？」

「交換？」大蟒蛇說，「嗯，我很喜歡這個家。不過，我應該可以拿它換一個更好的家。」

「什麼樣更好的家？」麥大虎問他。

「哦，一間用象草蓋的，既堅固又舒適的房子。」

「象草？」麥大虎說，「我怎麼用象草蓋房子呢？」

「我也不知道。你去問大象吧！」大蟒蛇說。

General MacTiger went down to the river to talk to the elephants, who were sloshing about there. They laughed **heartily** when they saw him. "Ho ho ho, you do look **comic**. Where are your **pajamas**?" they shouted.

General MacTiger thought that even without stripes he looked a lot smarter than the elephants. But this was no time to say so.

heartily [`hɑrtɪlɪ] 副 熱情地
comic [`kɑmɪk] 形 滑稽的
pajamas [pə`dʒæməz] 名 睡衣

So he just smiled **politely** and said, "**I was wondering if** you could help me with a little job. The thing is, I have to build a house for...ah, a friend of mine..."

"What friend?" said the **Chief** Elephant.

"Well, actually," said the General, "it's a snake I know. The...er...python."

politely [pə`laɪtlɪ] 副 禮貌地
I wonder if...　我不知道是否…
chief [tʃif] 形 首席的

　　於是麥大虎將軍就跑到河邊去找大象，大象正在河裡玩水。一看到麥大虎，大象們個個笑得合不攏嘴。
「呵、呵、呵，你的樣子好好笑。你的睡衣呢？」大象們說。

　　麥大虎將軍心想，雖然少了斑紋，他看起來還是要比那些笨大象聰明。不過現在可沒時間說這些了。

　　所以他只是很有禮貌地面露微笑。「不曉得你們願不願意幫我一點忙。事情是這樣子的，我必須替…嗯…一個朋友蓋間房子…」

　　「什麼朋友？」大象的頭頭問他。

　　「嗯，其實啊，」麥大虎吞吞吐吐的，「是我認識的一條蛇。就是…就是大蟒蛇。」

The Chief Elephant and all the other elephants laughed so hard that bunches of bananas came **thumping** down from the trees. Because they knew that the python had *no* friends, especially not the tiger.

"Very funny, I know," said General MacTiger. "But the fact is the python's got my stripes — you noticed I'm not wearing them today — and he'll only give them back if I build him a house. If you help me, maybe I can do something **in return**..."

thump [θʌmp] 動 發出砰砰聲
in return　回報

The General had no idea what he could do for the elephants; but the Chief Elephant said, "Well, there is one thing. We have a small problem with the **crocodiles**. They keep **straying** into our part of the river and sometimes we get **nasty bites** in the ankles. If you're such good friends with the python you're probably **pally** with the crocs too. I bet they'll do whatever you ask."

Then the elephants all laughed like a brass band and carried on **squirting** one another with water.

crocodile [`krɑkə,daɪl] 名 鱷魚
stray [stre] 動 漫遊
nasty [`næstɪ] 形 惡意的
bite [baɪt] 名 咬
pally [`pælɪ] 形 友好的
squirt [skwɝt] 動 噴水

　　大象聽了哈哈大笑，由於笑得太用力了，把成串成串的香蕉都震得掉到地上。因為大象知道大蟒蛇是沒有朋友的，更別說跟老虎作朋友了。

　　「我知道很好笑。」麥大虎說。「其實是大蟒蛇拿走了我的斑紋——你們應該也注意到我的斑紋不見了——他答應只要我幫他蓋間房子，就把斑紋還給我。如果你們能幫我的忙，或許我能做些什麼回報你們⋯⋯」

　　麥大虎其實也不曉得可以拿什麼回報大象。不過大象的頭頭說話了：「嗯，有一件事。我們和鱷魚之間有一點不愉快。他們老是闖入我們的地盤，有時候還朝我們的腳踝狠狠地咬下去。既然你能和大蟒蛇作朋友，和鱷魚打交道應該也沒問題。我敢說你的話他們絕不敢不聽。」

　　話一說完，一群大象笑成一團，簡直就像一支銅號樂隊。一隻隻大象還樂得朝空中噴起水來。

Standing well up on the riverbank, General MacTiger called down to the Grandmother of All the Crocodiles, who lay in the water like a log, with one **pebbly** eye open.

"Look here," said the General in an important voice. "You crocodiles have got to stay out of the elephants' part of the river, do you hear?"

pebbly [`pɛblɪ] 形（皮）有碎石花紋的

In a deep **creaky** voice, the Grandmother of All the Crocodiles said, "Why?"

General MacTiger thought for a moment and said, "Well, you know what elephants are — great **clumsy** things. They're afraid of **treading** on you."

He felt pleased with this **cunning** answer.

creaky [`krikɪ] 形 嘎吱作響的
clumsy [`klʌmzɪ] 形 笨手笨腳的
tread [trɛd] 動 踩踏
cunning [`kʌnɪŋ] 形 奸詐的

麥大虎站在河岸上，大聲呼叫鱷魚奶奶。鱷魚奶奶像塊木頭一樣趴在河裡，眼睛只有睜開一隻。

「聽著，」麥大虎故意裝做很神氣的樣子。「你們這些鱷魚從今以後不要再踏進大象的地盤。聽到了沒？」

鱷魚奶奶用低沉的破嗓子反問他：「為什麼？」

麥大虎想了一會兒才開口：「嗯，妳也知道大象笨手笨腳的，他們怕不小心會踩到你們。」

對於自己的小聰明，麥大虎好得意。

The Grandmother of All the Crocodiles looked at him without **blinking** for quite a long time. Then she said, "If the elephants are so worried about treading on us, why don't *they* move?"

The General had no answer to that, so he **huffed** and **puffed** and said, "Well, they aren't moving and that's that."

blink [blɪŋk] 動 眨眼
huff [hʌf] 動 發怒
puff [pʌf] 動 喘氣

The Grandmother of All the Crocodiles said in her creaky voice, "And if we move, what do we get?"

"Well, you won't get trodden on," said General MacTiger.

"That's what we shan't get. But what *shall* we get?" said the Grandmother of All the  Crocodiles.

"Doom and despair," thought the General, "where will this business end?"

　　鱷魚奶奶眼睛眨也不眨地看著他好一會兒，然後她說：「如果大象真的那麼擔心踩到我們，那他們為什麼不搬家？」

　　麥大虎這下子不知該怎麼回答，只好氣呼呼地對她說：「他們就是不想搬啦！」

鱷魚奶奶的破嗓子又說話了：「如果我們搬走，對我們有什麼好處？」
「這樣你們就不會被踩扁啊！」麥大虎說。
「我們是不會被踩到。可是我們能得到什麼好處？」鱷魚奶奶說。
「真慘，」麥大虎心想，「這下子沒完沒了了。」

Just at that moment down came a shower of coconuts, bop bop bop, one on each crocodile. "It's those monkeys again," said the Grandmother of All the Crocodiles. "They love dropping coconuts on us. Big joke, ha ha. If you stop them, then we might move."

"Stop the monkeys?" said the General.

"Right. Or else we stay put."

And she fell silent and lay as still as a log. When a crocodile stays put it really stays put.

"Fine," said General MacTiger, and **bounded** away. But he didn't know how he was going to **manage** this. Monkeys never do what anyone asks them to do. To begin with, he couldn't even see the monkeys, so he called out, "Monkeys! Are you there?"

bound [baʊnd] 動 彈跳
manage [ˋmænɪdʒ] 動 處理

　　就在這時候，從空中下好多椰子，嗶嗶波波地一個個打在鱷魚身上。「又是那群臭猴子，」鱷魚奶奶好生氣。「他們老愛拿椰子丟我們，以為這樣子很好玩。如果你能制止那群猴子，我們或許可以考慮搬走。」

　　「制止猴子？」麥大虎說。

　　「沒錯。否則我們就不走。」

　　說完，她就靜靜趴著，像塊木頭一樣動也不動。如果鱷魚說不動，那可真的是動也不動。

　　「好，」麥大虎將軍說完，轉身就走。可是他心裡一點主意也沒有。猴子是從不受人指揮的。更何況他現在連猴子的蹤影也看不到。於是他大叫起來：「猴子，你們在嗎？」

A shower of nuts and ripe fruit landed on him, so he knew the monkeys were there. He **wiped** himself clean and he said, "Now listen, monkeys —" But now the monkeys started **chattering** and **squeaking** so hard he couldn't hear himself speak, so he stopped. He didn't know what to say next anyway.

Now the General had another think, and when the monkeys' noise had **died down** a bit he said to himself, "Let me see if my thinking is right," and he called out, "Monkeys! Are you still there? I can't hear you any more!"

wipe [waɪp] 勔 擦抹
chatter [`tʃætɚ] 勔 嘰嘰喳喳
squeak [skwik] 勔 發吱吱聲
die down 減弱

　　突然，一大堆堅果和成熟的水果像雨點一樣打在他身上，原來猴子就在上面。他甩甩身體後對猴子說：「聽著，猴子⋯」沒想到這時猴子卻七嘴八舌、吱吱喳喳地吵了起來。麥大虎根本聽不到自己的聲音，最後乾脆閉上嘴巴。他不曉得接下來該說些什麼。

　　這時候麥大虎靈機一動。等到猴子安靜些後，他告訴自己：「我來看看我想得對不對。」於是他大聲叫了起來：「猴子，你們還在嗎？我怎麼聽不到你們的聲音？」

Now as soon as they heard this, the monkeys **shut up** completely. Silence fell on the forest. It was so silent that all the animals stopped what they were doing to listen to the silence. Bears, **boars**, **baboons**, bees and **beetles** all stood still and listened. It was the most unnatural and **unearthly** silence.

shut up　閉嘴

boar [bɔr] 名 野豬

baboon [bæ`bun] 名 狒狒

beetle [`bitl̩] 名 甲蟲

unearthly [ʌn`ɝθlɪ] 形 反常的

Then in the middle of the silence there was a small sound. It was the sound of General MacTiger laughing. Then gradually all the other forest noises started up again.

"Monkeys!" cried General MacTiger. "The crocodiles want to thank you for your kind gifts of coconuts. Please keep sending them. They love coconuts. Thank you, dear monkeys."

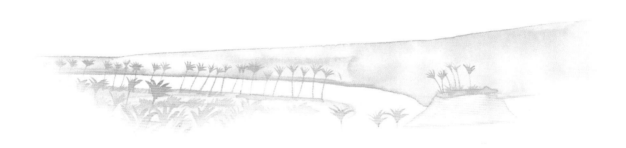

　　猴子一聽，立刻閉上嘴巴。森林瞬間安靜下來。因為太安靜了，所有動物也紛紛停了下來，仔細聽聽究竟發生了什麼事。熊、野豬、狒狒、蜜蜂、金龜子，全都停住不動。因為這安靜實在太奇怪了。

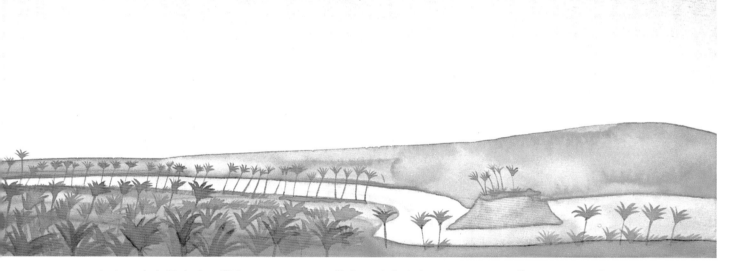

　　就在這一片安靜當中，響起了一個微小的聲音。原來是麥大虎將軍的笑聲。慢慢地，森林又開始吵雜了起來。

　　「猴子！」麥大虎將軍大聲喊叫。「鱷魚要謝謝你們常送他們椰子，請你們繼續再送椰子過去。他們很喜歡。謝謝你們，親愛的猴子。」

General MacTiger went to tell the crocodiles that the monkeys wouldn't be dropping any more coconuts on them. The Grandmother of All the Crocodiles opened her other eye and said, "How did you manage it?"

"Oh," said the General, "once you understand the monkeys they aren't so difficult."

So the crocodiles moved out of the elephants' water.

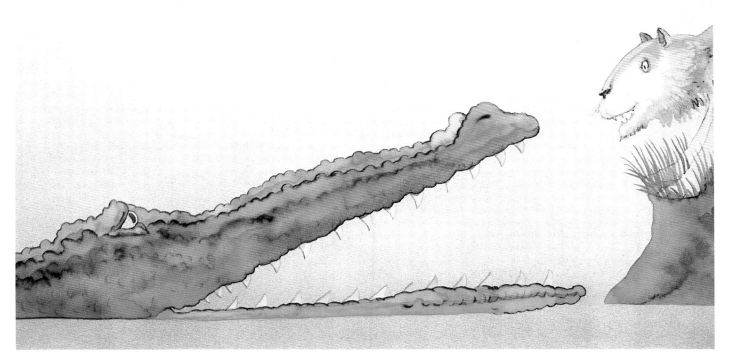

　　麥大虎將軍接著就跑去告訴鱷魚,說猴子以後不會再拿椰子丟他們了。鱷魚奶奶張開眼睛看著麥大虎說:「你怎麼辦到的?」

　　「哦,」麥大虎說,「如果妳了解猴子,會發現他們其實不難相處。」

　　於是鱷魚就搬離了大象的水域。

General MacTiger went to the elephants and said, "You see? The crocodiles have moved." The Chief Elephant made a **wheezy** noise like **leaking** bagpipes, and said, "How did you manage it?"

"Oh," said the General, "when you get to know the crocodiles they aren't so **crusty**."

wheezy [ˋhwizɪ] 形 喘息的
leak [lik] 動 漏
crusty [ˋkrʌstɪ] 形 暴躁的

　　麥大虎接著又跑去對大象說:「看到沒?鱷魚已經搬走了。」大象的頭頭一聽,發出呼嚕呼嚕的聲音,好像漏氣的風笛。他對麥大虎說:「你怎麼辦到的?」

　　「哦,沒什麼。」麥大虎說,「你只要了解鱷魚,就知道他們的脾氣其實沒那麼壞。」

So the elephants pulled up elephant grass and built a hut-thing. General MacTiger went to the python and said, "There's your new house. Now give me back my stripes."

The python liked the look of the hut-thing, so he slithered into it and let General MacTiger's stripes fall to the ground.

　　於是大象開始拔象草搭建小屋。麥大虎急忙跑去找大蟒蛇說：「這就是你的新家。現在可以把斑紋還給我了吧！」

　　大蟒蛇很喜歡那間小屋，於是滑呀滑地爬了進去，把麥大虎的斑紋甩在地上。

Quick as a flash, General MacTiger **untangled** the stripes and **put** them back **on**. Now he felt exactly like himself again, and started jumping about like a tiger kitten, until he remembered that he was General MacTiger, who was always dignified and stately.

untangle [ʌnˋtæŋgl̩] 動 解開
put...on 穿上⋯

　　麥大虎一看，飛也似地衝過去把斑紋解開套在身上。他覺得這個樣子才像真正的自己。麥大虎開心極了，蹦啊跳啊好像一隻小老虎，直到他想起自己是麥大虎將軍，永遠高貴、穩重的麥大虎將軍。

So he became **tremendously** stately, and **paraded** through the forest making sure that everything was just as it should be.

tremendously [trɪˋmɛndəslɪ] 副 非常地
parade [pəˋred] 動 裝模作樣地走路

　　於是他立刻安靜下來，擺出高貴、優雅的姿態，在森林裡四處巡視，要看看這世界是不是還跟以前一樣。

~ 看的繪本十聽的繪本　童話小天地最能捉住孩子的心 ~

為孩子寫～彩色的夢

 兒童文學叢書

·童話小天地·

嗯～磁鐵還滿好用，爸爸快快把屋的說故事時間就要開始囉！

國家圖書館出版品預行編目資料

失去斑紋的老虎 / Anthony Paul 著;Michael Foreman
繪;柯美玲譯.－－初版一刷.－－臺北市；三民，
民90
面；　公分－－(探索英文叢書)
ISBN 957－14－3402－7(平裝)

1.英國語言－讀本

805.18   90000774

網路書店位址　http://www.sanmin.com.tw

© 失去斑紋的老虎

著作人　　Anthony Paul
繪圖者　　Michael Foreman
譯　者　　柯美玲
發行人　　劉振強
著作財　　三民書局股份有限公司
產權人　　臺北市復興北路三八六號
發行所　　三民書局股份有限公司
　　　　　地址／臺北市復興北路三八六號
　　　　　電話／二五〇〇六六〇〇
　　　　　郵撥／〇〇〇九九九八——五號
印刷所　　三民書局股份有限公司
門市部　　復北店／臺北市復興北路三八六號
　　　　　重南店／臺北市重慶南路一段六十一號
初版一刷　中華民國九十年一月
　編　號　S 85508
　定　價　新臺幣壹佰玖拾元整
行政院新聞局登記證局版臺業字第〇二〇〇號

有著作權，不准侵害

ISBN　957　　　402　7　　（平裝）